This paperback edition first published in 2014 by Andersen Press Ltd.
20 Vauxhall Bridge Road, London SW1V 2SA.
First published in Great Britain in 1998 by Andersen Press Ltd.
Published in Australia by Random House Australia Pty.,
20 Alfred Street, Milsons Point, Sydney, NSW 2061.
Copyright © Foundation Max Velthuijs, 1998.
The rights of Max Velthuijs to be identified as the author and illustrator
of this work have been asserted by him in accordance with the
Copyright, Designs and Patents Act, 1988.
All rights reserved.
Colour separated in Switzerland by Photolitho AG, Zürich.
Printed and bound in China by Foshan Zhaorong Printing Co., Ltd.

10   9   8   7   6   5   4   3   2   1

British Library Cataloguing in Publication Data available.
ISBN 978 1 78344 148 8

This **Frog** book belongs to:

....

Frog
and the
Wide World

Max Velthuijs

Andersen Press

Rat stood on the top of a hill and looked out towards the horizon. "The world is quite beautiful," he sighed. And at once he felt restless. "It is time for me to go on my travels."

Early the next morning, he filled his rucksack
with things he might need, and provisions to
last him the journey.
Then he started on his way, eager for adventure.

He hadn't gone far when he heard a shout.

"Wait for me!"

He looked round, and saw Frog hurrying towards him.

"Rat!" said Frog. "Where are you going?"

"Out into the wide world," said Rat. "To seek adventure."

"May I come with you?" asked Frog in great excitement.
"Absolutely not!" exclaimed Rat. "You are far too small
for such a long journey."
"Oh, please, Rat. I'm small but I'm strong. I'll carry
things. And two is more fun than one."

"Come on, then," said Rat. "But don't fall behind!"
So together the two friends went out into the wide world.
Frog carried the rucksack and Rat led the way.
"This is pretty," said Frog after a while. "It's different
from home." He had never been so far afield before.

After they had walked a little further, Frog sat down.
"I'm hungry," he said. "When can we have lunch?"
"What?" exclaimed Rat. "We've only just started
our journey!"
All the same, he took two peanut-butter sandwiches
from the rucksack. He was ready for a bite to eat
himself. "It's only a snack, mind," he said sternly.
"We still have a long way to go."

When they had finished, they set out once more.
"Are we nearly there?" asked Frog.
"Where?" replied Rat.
"The wide world," said Frog.
"How can we be?" said Rat impatiently. "We've
hardly left home."

When they stopped walking, the sun had almost set. Frog collapsed on the ground. "I'm tired. I can't walk any further," he moaned. "When are we going home?" "Home?" Rat was astonished. "None of that! This is where we're going to spend the night."

Rat chose a comfy spot and they both lay down to rest.
"Rat," said Frog after a little while, "I can't sleep."
"Close your eyes and think of your favourite things,"
said Rat.
Frog tried but it didn't work. He could hear strange
noises. It was probably lions . . . or tigers.

When morning came, Frog didn't want to get up.
But Rat was firm, and off they set, up hill and down
dale, into the wide world. "Are we nearly there *now*?"
panted Frog.
"Not nearly," said Rat. "If you want to see anything
of the wide world you have to persevere."

Suddenly, the sky grew dark. The sun disappeared behind the clouds and it began to rain, softly at first but then harder and harder. The two friends rushed for shelter.

They were dry but Frog was cold.

"I wonder how things are at home," he said wistfully.

"I wonder how Pig is? And Duck and Hare?"

"The rain has stopped," said Rat. "Come on!"

They walked and walked until they came to some wild, deserted mountains. Up they clambered, over rocks and stones.
"Look at this! Isn't this fantastic?" called Rat.
But Frog had fallen, head over heels, and couldn't see anything.

"I think my foot is broken," wept Frog as he
stumbled on.
"It hurts so much, I can hardly walk."
"This will get us nowhere," grumbled Rat.
"From now on, I'll carry you."

He lifted Frog onto his back and marched on. "Perhaps Pig is baking a cake," said Frog. "And I wonder what Duck and Hare are doing? We always have such fun together, at home."

"You have the rest of your life to sit around at home," said Rat. "Right now, we're on our way to foreign lands. Look around you! See how beautiful it is? And everywhere is the unknown."

When at last they reached a grassy plane, Rat put
Frog down.
"I'm exhausted," he said. "We shall sleep here."
"Here?" asked Frog, dismayed. "At home I have
the best little bed in all the world . . ." But Frog
was tired, too, and he soon fell fast asleep.

But when they awoke the following morning, Frog just sat there in a miserable heap.
"Rat, I'm not well. I feel so ill. I don't want to go to the wide world. I miss home so much!"
"You're just too small for a trip around the world," said Rat. "You're not ill, you're homesick."

"Homesick?" Frog jumped up in alarm.
"Is that very bad?"
"Not very," said Rat. "You'll be better
once you're home."
"Home . . ." murmured Frog dreamily.
"That's it," said Rat "We're going back."

Frog didn't need to be carried any longer. He bounded on ahead, back to Pig and Duck and Hare. Rat had to laugh.

"Do you mind going back?" asked Frog.

"No, no," said Rat. "I was also missing home a bit. That's how it should be."

At last, after hours of walking, Frog gave a shout.
"Look! We're nearly there!"
And, sure enough, in the distance they saw Pig
and Duck and Hare waiting for them. Frog flew
towards his friends as if he had wings.

"Welcome home!" called Hare. "How was your trip?"
"Fantastic!" sang Frog. "The wide world is so
beautiful. And we've had such adventures. There
were lions and tigers and . . ."
"Come inside at once," said Pig, "and tell us all about
it. I have just baked a cake and you must be hungry."
That was just what Frog wanted to hear.

They sat around the table eating Pig's delicious
cake, while Frog described the terrible storm and
how brave they had been; the mountains they
had climbed and the sights they had seen.
"But there's still no place like home," said Frog,
and he thought happily to himself of his own,
nice, warm, little bed.

Max Velthuijs's twelve beautiful stories about **Frog** and his friends first started to appear twenty five years ago and are now available as paperbacks, e-books and apps.

9781783441440   9781783441532   9781783441501   9781783441426

9781783441471   9781783441457   9781783441525   97811783441433

9781783441518   9781783441495   9781783441488   9781783441419

Max Velthuijs (Dutch for Field House) lived in the Netherlands, and received the prestigious Hans Christian Andersen Medal for Illustration. His charming stories capture childhood experiences while offering life lessons to children as young as three, and have been translated into more than forty languages.

'Frog is an inspired creation — a masterpiece of graphic simplicity.' GUARDIAN

'Miniature morality plays for our age.' IBBY